Gene Kemp was born in Wigginton, a small Midland village outside Tamworth, whose famous pigs she celebrates in the *Tamworth Pig* stories, of which *Tamworth Pig and the Litter* is the third.

After several books about this wonderful pig and his friends, she broke new ground with her school story, *The Turbulent Term of Tyke Tiler*, which was awarded the Library Association's Carnegie Medal in 1978. In 1984 she was awarded an honorary Master of Arts degree in recognition of her achievement as a writer of children's books.

Gene Kemp now lives in Exeter. She is married with three children and has two grand-daughters.

**ff**

# TAMWORTH PIG AND THE LITTER

## Gene Kemp

*Illustrated by*
*Carolyn Dinan*

*faber and faber*
LONDON · BOSTON

First published in 1975
by Faber and Faber Limited
3 Queen Square London WC1N 3AU
This paperback edition first published in 1990

Printed in Great Britain by
Cox & Wyman Ltd, Reading, Berkshire
All rights reserved

A CIP record for this book is available from
the British Library

ISBN 0-571-14290-7

For Allan

# *Chapter One*

❖

Thomas stood and stared at the rain flowing down the window in an unbroken stream.

"Huh," he muttered. Then "Huh," he muttered again.

As if in sympathy the wind suddenly howled in a loud voice and buffeted its way round the house. Somewhere outside, a dustbin lid flew off, rattling down the garden path, and the shed door, that never would shut firmly, banged to and fro.

"Go and close that shed door, Thomas," called his mother from upstairs. He pretended not to hear. She came into the kitchen.

"Please go and shut the shed door," she said.

"You don't expect me to go out in that, do you?" he asked incredulously, waving a hand at the streaming window.

"Put something over your head, and slip your wellingtons on. And run. Before the shed blows away."

Groaning, Thomas did as he was told, and pushed open the kitchen door into a world of icy needles that stabbed his eyes, and shot instant wetness down his neck, and a wind that sent him staggering to the shed

even faster than he intended. Slamming the door, he ran back to the house and flung himself upon the sofa, grumbling.

"Saturdays! Saturdays! Misery days they should be called, not Saturdays. It's rained for the last six. It's not fair. It's just not fair. Why doesn't it rain when we're at school, that's what I'd like to know? But what happens? It waits till we want to play on Saturday, and then it comes down pouring in torrents, buckets, oceans. Huh!"

His mother spoke.

"Don't lie on the sofa with your wellingtons on. They're covered with mud and it's going all over the place. Take them off and put them away."

Thomas tugged at the boots, which seemed to be glued on to his feet, managed to pull them off, then threw them under the stairs, where they hit a packet of candles and a storm lantern, kept in case of power cuts, a box of tools, a tin of odds and ends, and two light bulbs in packets. They all fell down together. Thomas stirred the various objects with a somewhat grimy toe that was sticking out of his sock, then stomped upstairs to find his sister Blossom. She wasn't up to much, but she was better than nothing on a day like this. Little as the weather troubled him usually, the last few days of storm, wind, sleet and hail had prevented him from playing with his friend Henry, or his friend and rival, Lurcher Dench. He'd braved the storms once or twice to visit his oldest and best friend, Tamworth Pig, but even that seemed out of the question today.

Blossom looked up and smiled as he came in, her brown eyes shining. Rainy days held no terrors for her. She sat on the floor, surrounded by drawings, collages, a castle made from toilet rolls, a rag doll, a recorder and a large bag of toffees. Thomas helped himself to several of these.

"Look," she said, holding up her latest creation. It was an old-fashioned dolly's clothes peg, dressed in a striped poncho and a Mexican hat. She was painting in its face with a felt pen.

"He's Mexican Pete, and I'm going to make a desert with sand in that box, over there, and then shape some cactuses out of plasticine. I've already made a little Mexican house. Hacienda, I think it's called. . . .".

"Can't I make something?"

"Yes, you can draw a face on this one."

She handed him a peg and some felt pens. Thomas drew a face: two eyes, a nose, mouth, chin, ears and hair.

"What about that?"

Blossom snorted and dropped the doll she was working on.

Thomas looked indignant.

"What's wrong? What are you laughing for? It's all right, isn't it?"

Blossom choked back a giggle.

Puzzled, Thomas looked at the face he'd drawn. What was the stupid girl carrying on like that for? What was the matter? Perhaps it didn't look quite right. Perhaps the eyes were too near the top of the head or too close together, and perhaps the mouth shouldn't stretch from one ear to the other. He dropped it on the floor.

"Forget it. I'll make a cactus plant instead."

He softened and rolled the green and yellow plasticine in his hands. It felt warm and soft and gooey and he knew it was time to start shaping it. He'd never been any good at drawing faces, but he was sure he could make a marvellous cactus, with long, sharp spikes sticking out of it.

They worked together in silence, Blossom spreading sand in the bottom of the box, and Thomas creating a cactus.

"There." He held it out for her to see. "It's finished."

There was a pause.

"Let me put it in the sand," Thomas said.

Blossom got between him and her model.

"What's wrong with it?" Rumblings of fury threatened in Thomas's voice. "It's good."

"Yes. It is. But it's too big."

"They are big. In the desert, that is. They're not the nitty, squidgy things you see in pots here, stupid. . . ."

"I know that. But it doesn't fit in with the other things. It's three times as big as the houses are going to be. Make it smaller, please."

"No, I won't. It's smashing as it is and I'm not altering it for you or anyone else."

"Just as you like, but I don't want it that size."

She smiled at Thomas hopefully, praying that he wouldn't get into one of his furies. But too late.

"I don't want anything to do with you or any of your stupid rubbish, you great fat idiot," he bellowed, up-ending the box of sand over Blossom's head. He then rushed out of the room and down to the kitchen, where he seized a packet of biscuits out of the cupboard and ripped off the wrapping. Most of the biscuits broke in half and fell on the floor. He kicked them further on their way, then changed his mind, and picked up the fragments. They were somewhat tatty, but after wiping them on the seat of his jeans, he scrunched them loudly and reached out for the bottle of orange juice. He filled a glass nearly to the brim before he added water, and then had to throw half away because it was too strong. Wiping up the orange pool with his elbow, he sighed and looked out of the window, where the rain still descended from the grey sky.

His mother appeared at the door. "What have you been doing to Blossom? She's crying. And what have you done to this floor? What do you think you're . . . ?"

Thomas stopped listening to this barrage of questions. He knew the rest. He'd heard it all before. Funny, really. Mum was all right, but she would go on and on and on.

"Can I have five pence to spend?" he asked, when she paused for breath. But she revved up like a car starting off and began again. Thomas understood that he had to help Blossom clear up the sand, tidy his room, and did he think she was some sort of slave?

"No, I don't think you're some sort of slave," said Thomas. "It's not Roman times."

For some reason she looked as if she was going to explode, but the door bell rang, and Thomas rushed for it, hoping it might be one of his friends braving the storms to visit him. But no; there, fully prepared against the weather in flowered mackintosh, umbrella and boots, stood Gwendolyn Twitchie, friend of Blossom and the daughter of Thomas's Headmistress. Even though her yellow, corkscrew curls were tucked neatly into a waterproof hood, the mere sight of her was enough to make Thomas feel ill.

"Urgh!" He made a sick sort of noise, slammed the door, and turned away. His mother stood right behind him.

"Thomas! Don't be so rude. What a thing to do. Shutting someone outside on a day like this."

She opened the door. "Come in, Gwendolyn. Go up and tidy your room, Thomas."

"What a life. What a miserable life. I might as well be dead or in a dungeon," Thomas grumbled as he went upstairs. Once in his room, he kicked under the bed several paperbacks, some shoes, pencils, two crisp bags and a box of Lego. Seizing a very old Beano, he flung himself down and started to read.

Mr. Rab and Hedgecock were arguing as usual at the bottom of the bed. Mr. Rab was a long thin rabbit who looked as if he'd been stretched at some time. He had a pink nose, the colour of raspberry blancmange. He loved poetry and gentleness and Blossom and detested Hedgecock, who was a cantankerous old animal with feathery prickles. No one really knew what he was, and since he was very touchy on the subject, it was best not to ask.

"Stop mumbling to yourself," he was saying to Mr. Rab.

"I'm not mumbling. I'm making up an epic poem. It begins:

'The mighty Tamworth, he of giant form

One night awoke from dreams distraught and wild.'"

"Ow, shut up. Lord, love a duck, what a load of old muck." Hedgecock was rather a common animal. "Give me numbers any time," he went on. "Nine elevens are ninety-nine is far better than any poem." He fixed Mr. Rab with his bright, beady eyes. "Besides, what's an epic poem when it's at home?"

"It's a very long and grand one," Mr. Rab said stiffly.

"Long and grand balderdash, you mean."

Mr. Rab turned his back on Hedgecock, who continued:

"Why don't you do something useful? Like decimals, for instance."

Mr. Rab swung round, his nose a-quiver.

"I don't like decimals or think they are any use at all. The world would be a far better place without them. Think of all those unhappy children at school being forced to LEARN DECIMALS!" Mr. Rab's voice, which had risen higher and higher, ended with a loud shriek as Hedgecock kicked him.

"You silly, striped thing, why, we'd still be living in caves and up trees if it weren't for inventors and scientists and mathematicians. And they mostly used decimals."

"What does it matter where we live? The important thing is to spread love and beauty around us, like Blossom and me."

Hedgecock laughed so much that he fell off the bed and all his feathery prickles got ruffled. Thomas leaned over and scooped him off the floor.

"That serves you right. Now shut up, and listen. I think this rain is going to last for ever, so I want to think who we are going to have in our Ark, because we shall have to build one."

"Me."

"Me."

"Oh, yes, you two. And Tamworth and Melanie and the piglets, and Mum to do the cooking, and Dad, perhaps, I suppose. But not Gwendolyn Twitchie. Nor Blossom. . . ."

"We've got to have Blossom. She's the nicest person in all the world."

"She'll have to keep to the other side of the Ark, then. And I'll have Joe the shire horse, and Barry MacKenzie Goat, but I won't have Mrs. Twitchie. I hope she and Gwendolyn die a long, lingering, drowning death."

Mr. Rab was sobbing. "I don't like to think of the world drowning. I'd get wet."

"You're wet already," Hedgecock growled.

"I wish there was something to do. I'm bored, BORED," Thomas cried. He lay across the bed, head and arms hanging one side, legs and feet the other. He saw Blossom's tennis ball lying with many other things under the bed. He hadn't the faintest idea how it had got there. He flipped it out and began to dribble it round the room with great care. He wasn't supposed to play football in the house—not after the two windows he broke last month—but he just couldn't resist kicking it one more time. He passed to Hedgecock, and then tackled him and retrieved it again.

"Nice one, Thomas," he sang out. "I'm going to shoot," and swung his leg and kicked, no, not hard, not hard at all. Through the window flew the ball; there was a tinkle, a hole, a spreading of cracks like a spider's web as out flew the ball and in flew the wind and rain, joined by a shower of glass splinters.

"Oh, Oh, Oh," cried Mr. Rab.

Silence fell. They sat still for what seemed a long time. Then "Mum," called Thomas, and then "Mum" again.

"What is it?" she called. "I'm busy."

"You'd better come and see."

Thomas sat on the bed and fished out Num, his old grey blanket. He wrapped it round himself to keep off the world outside and all the trouble thereof. Mr. Rab and Hedgecock huddled beside him, Hedgecock reciting the nine times table as fast as he could.

Later on in the day, after Blossom had helped him to fix some cardboard over the broken window, which was not easy because of the rain, and Thomas had decided she was not too bad after all for she always helped him no matter how much they fell out, and Daddy had looked at it, and said "Humph, what again?" the wind dropped and the rain stopped and the sun came out among the clouds. A rainbow formed over the telephone wires.

Inside Thomas a bubble of happiness pushed away the gloom. Grabbing Hedgecock and Mr. Rab, he rushed outside. The air was fresh with spring, the grass glistened, and leaves were starting to push out of the brown buds, stirred by the light breeze.

Kicking an old rubber ball that just happened to be in the path, and singing, "Nice one, Thomas," at the top of his voice, he rushed off to see Tamworth Pig.

# Chapter Two

---
❖
---

"The naming of piglets is a very important affair. A name can make a piglet or break a piglet. A piglet has a better chance of growing into a fine, noble pig if he has the right name, the name that suits him. All my life I have been helped by the name Tamworth, which is just right for me. And so, dear friends, I have the most enormous and tremendous pleasure in welcoming you to this happy occasion, the naming of the piglets."

Tamworth stood in front of Pig House, under the damson tree, now starry with blossom. Huge and golden in colour, with a long snout and furry, upstanding ears, he was the biggest and best-known pig in the British Isles, President of the Animals' Union, and Organizer of the campaigns to "Grow More Grub", and "Save The Trees". He knew and was known by many famous people, but here at home he was Thomas's friend and the father of twenty piglets. Today they were to be given their names, and they all stood beside Melanie, their small black and pink mother. The littlest of the litter was there, now grown almost as big as the others. Tamworth had given him the kiss of life when he was born, because he was so weak, but now he was twice as tough and three times as cheeky as all the others.

Tamworth finished speaking and the audience clapped. Blossom and Thomas were there, with Hedgecock and Mr. Rab, Lurcher and Henry, Mummy with her friends, the Vicar's wife and Mrs. Postlewaithe, Joe the shire horse, Fanny Cow, Barry MacKenzie Goat, Ethelberta Everready the champion egg-layer, and many others, including Owly, who was having trouble trying to stay awake in the strong morning light. And the Welsh Rabbit had come in from the Tumbling Wood with a bunch of wild flowers from the animals who lived there, and whose homes had been saved by Tamworth.

In front of the great pig stood a white bowl, filled with water, into which the falling petals from the damson tree drifted gently. Farmer Baggs, who owned Tamworth and the piglets, held the little animals over the bowl, while Tamworth sprinkled some drops of water on each snout. Mrs. Baggs, the farmer's wife, was not present, since she detested Tamworth and anything to do with him, which included Melanie and the piglets.

These were their names: first Michael, a golden pig, just like his father, and Melanie's favourite, then Percy, Spotty, Spendergast, Antony, Daisy, Julius Caesar, Harry Grunter, Jennyanydots, Agatha, Windy, Jenkins, Marmalade, Ethel, Bruno, Bomber, George Biscuit, Gopherson and Pillowcase. Just then, the black runt, who hated being left till last, gave a loud squeal and jumped straight into the water, splashing everyone. The bowl overturned and away rolled the little pig.

Thomas rolled about too, with laughter.

"Oh, dear," cried Melanie. "He's always in trouble. Always in hot water."

"It's cold, not hot." Thomas laughed even louder. Others started to join in. Tamworth picked up the piglet ignoring all the disturbance.

"I shall call you Albert," he pronounced, "after that wise and noble pig, my father, whom I remember well."

Albert hiccupped.

"I can't think why they've got all those names," Hedgecock grumbled. "Numbers would have been much better."

"Names have poetry in them," protested Mr. Rab.

"Fat lot of poetry there is in a name like Spotty, I must say," Hedgecock scoffed.

"Now for the celebration," cried Tamworth. "Come on. Tuck in."

A trestle table had been set up beside Pig House, with a fine white cloth on it, and there had been placed eggs, salmon, tomatoes, lettuces, mushrooms, long loaves and butter, frozen strawberries and cream, doughnuts, apple tart, cheese straws, biscuits, peanuts, crisps, apples, oranges and bananas, liquorice allsorts, Pig's Delight, wine, beer, cider, coke and lemonade. But there was no pork or ham or sausages, for Tamworth would not allow these foods anywhere near him. For those with plainer tastes, like Joe, there were hay and water and some sugar lumps. Blossom made hay in a different fashion. She ate as much as possible. Tamworth partook of his favourite brand of cabbage, a few apples and lots of beer. Daddy, who had been working, now arrived, and the Vicar's wife brought out paper hats and balloons. Soon they were dancing round the table singing lots of jolly songs, such as "Here we go round the mulberry bush", "Save the Trees", and "Nice one, Tamworth, Nice one, Son". Farmer Baggs and Daddy did not join in the singing, as they were very busy seeing that none of the beer was wasted.

At last the piglets fell asleep in unlikely places and peculiar positions and were carried inside to be placed in their box, where they snuffled and grunted and kicked their piggy trotters as they dreamed their piggy dreams. All their stomachs were as round and hard as barrels, Thomas noted as he rubbed them.

"Mine's hard and round as well," Blossom groaned. "I ate too much."

The guests departed, leaving Thomas and Blossom. It was still quite early in the day. Rather slowly, for it was difficult to bend down, they helped Tamworth clear up all the remains and the rubbish till it was tidy again under the damson tree. Blossom put a few left-over delicacies aside for emergencies. Melanie settled down beside the piglets.

"Suppose we take a walk, dear friends," Tamworth suggested. "Where shall we go?"

"To the stream. I want to get some water-snails and some weed for the aquarium at school," Thomas answered.

"There might be some baby frogs, I think," Blossom said. "It's the right time of the year for them."

"The stream, then."

Moving slowly, for they were still rather full, they set off for the Common. The grassy turf was springy with crumbled brown mole hills here and there. The air smelt of spring and all good things, and soon Thomas was racing along at terrific speed, followed more slowly by the rest. It was some time since he had been to the stream, and he wanted to see if it had changed much.

It had.

A number of bottles, some broken, squeezy cartons, crisp bags, cigarette packets, soup tins, buckets, yards of rusty chicken wire and a holey vest lay in the water, which looked dark and scummy.

"Ugh." Blossom pulled a face. "Look at that. Talk about pollution."

"If any more rubbish is dumped in, the stream will be blocked up and that will flood the moles out of their holes," Tamworth said, perturbed.

"You mean like Thomas did once," put in Mr. Rab.

"And you. You were there, too," Hedgecock said, giving him a kick to remind him.

"Shut up. If I'm to get any snails and stuff from here we'd better clear it first," Thomas said, taking off his shoes and socks, which were his best ones, worn for the party. Slime clung round his bare legs.

"This bucket will be useful," he shouted, then, quick as a flash, he threw an old hat at Blossom, who shrieked and dropped it. Mud oozed down her coat.

"I think I shall join you," Tamworth cried, leaping in with a splash that sprayed everything within the nearest twenty yards. Blossom gave up trying to keep clean and dry, took off her boots and socks and joined in as well. So did Hedgecock, and they were soon clearing the stream of litter and piling it on to the banks. All except one of them, that is.

"Why aren't you in here, pink nose?" Hedgecock asked. "Come and get stuck in like the rest of us."

"You know how easily I catch cold. I'm not rough and tough like you," sniffed Mr. Rab.

"You lazy, good-for-nothing-layabout," bellowed Hedgecock, splashing violently. "Just you come and help or I—will—come—and—get—you!"

Mr. Rab scurried into the water, eeking pitifully as it swirled round his skinny legs. Shuddering, he picked up a jam jar.

"Poets aren't meant to do this kind of thing," he wailed.

"Poets! Pooh!" Hedgecock jeered, upending the contents of an old bean tin over the shivering form. In the tin were some minute water creatures who thought the

end of the world had come and so it nearly had for them, but they returned to the stream, surprised but surviving.

Next, Thomas splashed Hedgecock.

"Behave yourselves in a seemly fashion," Tamworth commanded, but the words turned into a whistling snort that made Thomas sit down in the cocoa-brown water. He jumped up speedily, for it was wintry cold. Blossom laughed with glee. And at that moment who should trip by, all neat and trim, but Mrs. Twitchie and Gwendolyn.

They nodded coolly and went on their way. By a trick of the wind their voices carried back clearly.

"I don't think they should have been causing all that mess. I must say I'm surprised at Tamworth Pig," said Mrs. Twitchie.

"Sometimes Blossom seems rather dirty and common, I think," put in Gwendolyn.

Blossom's feelings were hurt, but Thomas couldn't stop laughing.

"She's common on the Common," he shouted.

"I don't think that's at all funny. I'm going home," snapped his sister.

"So are we all," Tamworth said, emerging from the stream like a great whale. "I'll come back later with Joe the shire horse to clear this away. And we'll come back again tomorrow to see how the stream is and keep it clear."

Actually it was a week before they returned to the stream. Mummy had had a lot to say about their ways when they went back home.

# Chapter Three

❖

Blossom looked up from her magazine.

"They're offering a prize for the best poster on keeping the countryside free from litter. I think I'll do one. Anybody got any ideas?"

Thomas didn't take much notice. He was busy taking a clockwork engine to pieces to see how it worked. He often did this and then was annoyed when he couldn't put it back together again.

"What about 'Litter is Foul'?" suggested Hedgecock, for he remembered seeing something like that somewhere.

Mr. Rab giggled. "Fowls don't have litters, silly. They lay eggs. Animals have litters. Like Melanie and the piglets."

Here he stopped, for Hedgecock was glaring at him, feathery prickles erect.

"It's you that's silly. There are two kinds of litter, you pink-nosed, dimwitted, poetry-writing. . . ."

"Shush," interrupted Blossom, "I've got an idea. Let me think." After a minute she jumped up. "I've got it. Thanks, you two. You've given me the idea. I know what to draw."

"I'm going to do one as well," said Thomas, dropping

the remains of the engine behind the sofa. "Lend me your black felt pen."

"*No*," Blossom answered, going out of the room.

"Why not?" He followed her.

"Because I've kept all mine safe in the cupboard, and my paints and crayons, while you've used yours for swords and all sorts of things like sticking in plasticine, and so now you want mine. No."

"You're a rotten ole meanie."

"No, I'm not."

"Meanie. Meanie."

"Now what's the matter?" asked their mother, coming down the stairs as they made their quarrelling way up.

"Blossom won't share her felt pens with me."

"Oh, Blossom. You know I have always told you we must share our things with others. That's what life is all about."

Blossom went crimson.

"What life is all about is Thomas spoiling everything I ever want to do," she shouted and ran into the bedroom, banging the door behind her. Her mother followed. Blossom was sobbing into the floppy doll that Tamworth Pig had once given her. Jemima, she was called.

"What's the matter. Blossom?"

Blossom dried her eyes on Jemima's rather grubby apron and sat up.

"It's all right, now. He can use my things. I don't really mind."

Thomas stood in the doorway, grinning. Blossom turned to him.

"I still think you're horrible," she said.

Thomas's grin grew even wider.

They spread newspaper on the floor and began. An hour later Blossom's poster was ready. Its colours were black, white, pink and gold and it showed the piglets picking up rubbish with their snouts and trotters, and putting it in bins. Across it was written, "Help with Litter". It was a handsome poster. Blossom's hair stood on end and her fingers were all podged out of shape where she had held the pens so tightly, but her eyes shone. Sighing with satisfaction, she looked at what Thomas had done.

"What is it?" she asked. Thomas scowled. His face was covered in black marks. He only liked using black and, occasionally, red.

"It's an invention. A litter-picking machine. But it hasn't come out right."

"What a clever idea. I'd never have thought of that." Blossom sat back on her heels to inspect it thoroughly.

"It's a mess, a horrible mess. I hate drawing. My drawings never say what they've got to say."

Thomas's picture was all smudges and rumples, because he'd changed his mind half-way and rubbed everything out before beginning again. He slammed out of the room. Slowly, Blossom cleared up the debris, still thinking of his picture.

"It's a brilliant idea. Now if . . . I drew it neatly . . . only . . . he'd be angry if I did. . . ."

She sat down and, taking a fresh piece of paper, started to copy the litter machine, leaving out all the mistakes.

Meanwhile Thomas jumped, hopped, leapt and bounded down the stairs, touching one in three, then charged out of the house like an enraged buffalo.

"Close the door," came a cry from behind him but he didn't hear.

Lurcher Dench was in the street, kicking stones down a drain, and noting which ones were too big to go down. He spotted Thomas and called out:

"What have you been doing? Tattooing yourself?"

Instantly Thomas felt that everything was Lurcher's fault, so he strode over and hit him on the chest. Lurcher lashed out with his fist, then hooked one leg round Thomas's so that he fell over. Thomas's hand shot up and he pulled Lurcher on top of him, where they rolled about pummelling each other.

"Now, then, you two." The boys found themselves in mid-air, kicking uselessly. P.C. Cubbins shook them once or twice, then stood them back on the ground.

"Off you go and play somewhere, instead of fighting. No good ever came of fighting. Now shake hands, you hooligans."

They shook hands. P.C. Cubbins grinned. It was a good thing that he had caught them and not P.C. Spriggs, who thought the worst of everyone, especially children. He detested Thomas particularly, but he didn't much care for Lurcher either. The boys shook themselves as the constable left them.

"What shall we play?" Thomas asked.

"Football."

"No, cricket."

"Cricket, then."

"Haven't got a ball. Crasher took it." Crasher was one of the many Dench brothers.

"Blossom's got a new tennis ball. Wait."

Back into the house crept Thomas as silently as he had gone out noisily. Under the stairs he found Blossom's ball, all fluffily white as new tennis balls are.

He rejoined Lurcher and they went down to the Common. The clouds sailed fat and white and fluffy in the blue sky, rather like Blossom's ball, in fact. They played with Lurcher's old bat, with a tree for the wicket. It was a jolly good game. Thomas had scored fifty-eight when Lurcher sent down a slow, high googly. Thomas stepped forward and slammed it hard, up and up, away, into the air, into the wild blue yonder and then straight down into the middle of the stream, which was really a fair distance from where they were playing. Both boys ran to the bank, and saw the ball floating ahead of them, in the clear-running water. On they ran, to see the ball drop plop over a waterfall and into the narrower, deeper stream beyond. They had almost caught up with it. Then at exactly the same moment, like performing twins, they both leapt off the bank into the stream, colliding with each other, banging heads and falling in. The white ball sailed on smugly till it came to rest at a tiny sandy bay in a curve of the stream.

They picked up themselves and then the ball. A lump was forming on Lurcher's forehead and Thomas had a cut lip. They shook themselves like wet spaniels and set off for home.

"You know," Thomas remarked as they squelched along, "I shall get told off for fighting you and taking her ball, when, really, we were just trying to save it." Some time later he sat by Tamworth, stroking the furry ears. The piglets lay over them like a warm, breathing blanket.

"Huh. I've got to buy her a new ball with my pocket-money," he muttered into the ears, which twitched a little.

"Justice must be done and must be seen to be done, dear boy," Tamworth murmured sleepily.

"Justice ought to be on my side all the time. That's what I think," Thomas replied.

"But that's what everyone thinks, and that's what causes trouble," yawned Tamworth and, like the piglets, fell asleep.

# Chapter Four

❖

Some weeks later Tamworth was invited to take the morning Assembly at school. This pleased him greatly and he put on his new, black-rimmed spectacles for the first time, balancing them with loving care on his snout. He was very proud of them. So was Melanie.

"You're the handsomest pig in the whole world, and you look even handsomer in your spectacles," she told him. Tamworth nodded as he gazed at himself in the mirror. He heartily agreed with her, but feared it might sound too conceited if he actually said so.

In the school hall, he told the children to sit down, and they were as quiet as mice while he talked to them about the best of saints, Saint Francis, who loved all animals, all living things, in fact, who treated them as his friends and called them brothers, and how he tamed the fierce wolf so that he became gentle and loving. Saint Francis was a good man. He would have made an excellent pig, Tamworth concluded. Mrs. Twitchie, who had invited him, looked surprised at this remark, but she thanked him warmly for coming. She'd been in a very good mood lately.

Everyone stood up to sing "All creatures of our God

35

and King," which is Saint Francis's hymn, and the
school orchestra joined in, loud and jollily. Blossom
played her violin, a serious and solemn expression on
her face. Thomas felt like throwing something at her.
Then he looked at Tamworth on the platform and felt
proud. The best pig in the world, he thought.

After they had sung "We wish you many happy
returns of the Day," to Crasher Dench, whose birthday
it was, Mrs. Twitchie held up her hand. There was
instant silence.

"I'm delighted to announce that Blossom has won
first prize in a Keep the Countryside Tidy competition.
I shall ask Tamworth Pig to present her with the prize."

Noise filled the hall as the hands clapped, all except one pair of hands. Thomas sat silent, staring at the floor, his eyes slits of jealousy. The other prizes went to other schools. Blossom had indeed done well.

Blossom went forward from the orchestra, her face scarlet, brown eyes shining, and fell over one of the music stands. Laughter mingled with the clapping and her face turned redder still.

"Sorry," she mumbled. Tamworth beamed with delight, glowing like a huge sun upon the platform, as he handed her not just one prize, but a huge drawing book, a box of poster paints, a set of tubes, a box of felt tips and a book token.

And Thomas's thoughts were black as coal, black as night, black as black holes in space. Nothing was fair, nothing was ever fair. Why should she get a prize for her stupid painting? She'd be insufferable. In utter gloom he trailed out of the hall. All day he sat, dreary and despondent, stuffing his hands over his ears and speaking to no one. Henry tried to show him his new Dinky car but Thomas ignored him and the car. He did his work and no more. Lurcher came up to yell "Good ole Blossom," in his ear, and Thomas snarled and would have kicked him, but that Mr. Starling, their teacher, came in just then.

At the end of school he dawdled home, alone, dragging his feet. The day that had begun with such promise with Tamworth telling them about Saint Francis had turned into misery as Blossom's poster was hung in a position of honour. It was too much.

He knew just what it would be like at home. Mummy

would laugh and hug her and Daddy would say funny things, but he would be pleased just the same. And all those horrible girls would call round and squeak and squawk:

"Oh, how absolutely fabulous!"

"You're so clever!"

"Draw me a picture. Please."

Slowly he entered the house and looked into the living room. Just as he had thought, it was full of people looking at the prizes. Slowly he went upstairs. He lay on the bed, head hanging over one side, feet over the other, face in Num, the comforter, Mr. Rab and Hedgecock clutched to him. They knew better than to speak to him, for Thomas in a fury was bad, but Thomas in a black mood was worse. It was best to wait till things grew better again. After a time he spoke.

"Nobody wanted my invention picture. They only care about her, that's all. Her and her rotten picture. Tamworth as well. He's just as bad."

Getting to his feet, he wandered downstairs. No one seemed to be about now. He felt hungry. Wasn't anyone ever going to get a meal? As far as he could see no one cared whether he had anything to eat or not. He could starve and no one would bother. He might as well be dead or in a dungeon. He looked in the living room. It was empty. Everyone had disappeared. On the table lay pots and tubes of paint beside the drawing book. The book token was not there, though. Gone to spend it, I suppose, he thought bitterly.

In utter silence Thomas walked to the table and unscrewed the tops of the tubes of paint. They came off surprisingly easily. Then he squeezed them all over the beautiful, clean pages of the drawing book. Black and green, purple and blue, red and yellow; he swirled the colours together, then closed up the book. Squodges of multi-coloured paint oozed thickly out of the sides.

Still in (utter) silence, he walked out of the house, into the garden and then to the Common. The late afternoon was calm and still. He saw no one. Thomas lay down on his stomach in the grass and hid his face among the green blades, and watched all the busy dwellers of the strange grass world. A wind got up and ruffled the leaves. It grew cooler, and he shivered. He was very hungry. He wanted his tea. He wanted to go home, but he didn't think he could ever go home again. He didn't suppose they would want him to go home again. Far away he heard voices and he looked up eagerly but no one came. He wanted Mummy, yes, and Daddy. He wanted Tamworth. He even wanted Blossom. He wanted to say he was sorry. A tear trickled down his face and dropped on a long-legged spider that scuttled even more quickly through the grass. Still no one came to look for him. Didn't anybody care? Soon it would be dark, he was sure. He sat up. He didn't want to be alone and hungry on the Common.

Slowly he stood up and went back home.

He pushed open the kitchen door. There they were, Mummy and Daddy and Blossom. He put his hands together tight behind his back and said all-in-a-rush:

"I'm very sorry. Really."

She'd been crying. Her face was all blotchy.

She held out a parcel for him.

"I bought that book for you. The one you wanted on wild animals."

And she burst into tears. Mummy was crying too.

Daddy jumped up. "For goodness sake. It's like a wet Bank Holiday here. Cheer up, all of you, and then we can think up a new set of resolutions for Thomas on how to be a better boy!"

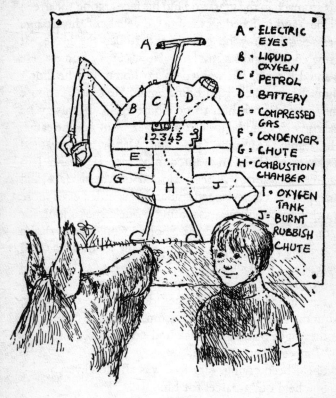

A = ELECTRIC EYES
B = LIQUID OXYGEN
C = PETROL
D = BATTERY
E = COMPRESSED GAS
F = CONDENSER
G = CHUTE
H = COMBUSTION CHAMBER
I = OXYGEN TANK
J = BURNT RUBBISH CHUTE

Next day he went to see Tamworth, who was admiring a new picture on the wall. Thomas took a second look at it, for it somehow seemed familiar. Yes, it was. The litter-picking invention looked back at him, but neater and tidier than he remembered.

"Where did you get that?"

"I asked Blossom for it. She brought it to show me, because she thought it was brilliant. And I must say I agree with her. Drawing's easy if you happen to have a gift for it, but it takes brains to invent things."

Tamworth's eyes twinkled and he wore a wide, curly grin.

"You could be right," Thomas nodded modestly.

Blossom, coming up to Pig House just behind him, found all the piglets in the orchard gathering round Albert, who was wearing an old grey blanket.

"What are you doing?" she asked, for all the others were listening most solemnly to him.

"Me?" squeaked Albert. "Why, I'm Saint Francis talking to his brother animals. Them."

He waved a lordly trotter over his brothers and sisters and they all nodded together.

# Chapter Five

✦

Tamworth sat at his desk reading one of the many letters that he received daily, when Thomas came in with the piglets, who flopped down on the floor and fell asleep immediately, for they were exhausted from trying to play football. Michael the eldest, was getting the idea very nicely, but a certain black one had been sent off by Thomas, because he kicked the others instead of the ball or tried to trip them up. Thomas sent him to sit under the damson tree, where he pulled snouts and fidgeted till the game was over. Then he had run to Thomas and rubbed against him so that he was forgiven. Now, like the rest, he was fast asleep.

In the peace and quiet Tamworth said to Thomas:

"The Vicar's wife has been to see me."

Thomas helped himself to some Pig's Delight and mumbled:

"What about?"

"She wants to start a Keep Tidy campaign in the village. She thought we could use some posters like Blossom's. . . ." Here he paused and peered closely at Thomas to see if he was still feeling jealous, then added:

". . . and she admired your invention very much, too."

Thomas's mouth was too crammed with Pig's Delight for him to say anything, so Tamworth continued:

"She appears to have an abundance of ideas and wants us to deliver these notices about holding a meeting. So, old chap, just leap on my back and off we trot."

The following week, everybody who was or thought themselves to be of any importance attended the school hall. When it was full, the Vicar's wife asked Tamworth to speak. He put on his spectacles and looked round the hall.

"Friends and brothers, not long ago I went to the Common in order to walk by the stream which I have always loved, and what did I see?"

Here he paused and Mrs. Dench, who dearly loved to say a word, too, opened her mouth, but Mr. Dench poked her with his elbow, so she closed it again. Tamworth continued:

"Instead of clear, rippling, silvery water singing over the shining stones, I saw slimy, scummy, polluted mud, frothing and oozing over vile unspeakable rubbish, tins, bottles, bags, cartons and bones."

"I don't remember any bones," whispered Thomas.

"Shush," hissed Blossom.

Tamworth was going well now.

"Nothing to be seen, but detritus. Detritus," he bellowed, very pleased with the word, which is why he had said it twice. Not more than half a dozen people in the room had ever heard it before, but a little cheer went up from the back row. Tamworth lowered his voice and looked down his spectacles.

". . . and now—wherever I go, I look around me and what do I see?"

"Piglets?" suggested Henry's father, the Professor, who hadn't been listening properly.

"Rubbish," roared Mrs. Dench, getting her word in at last.

"Yes, indeed," Tamworth answered her, trying hard not to think of the Dench garden, which held more rubbish than the rest of the entire neighbourhood.

"I know. Litter!" It was the voice of Mrs. Twitchie, getting everything right.

Tamworth leaned forward from the platform.

"I do hope he doesn't fall off," Blossom thought, anxiously, "or the people in the front row will get squashed." Thomas was thinking the same, only he rather hoped it might happen.

"And so, my friends, we have come here tonight to see if we can do anything about this state of affairs. Has anyone any ideas?"

Tamworth sat down and there was silence. No one said a word and the seconds crawled by like snails.

"Why doesn't someone speak?" Blossom thought desperately, going red with panic.

The Vicar's wife brought out a paper from her bag.

"It looks like a sheet of music. What on earth is she doing with a sheet of music?" Blossom wondered.

The Vicar's wife stood up, and smiled her wide, gentle smile.

"While you all think up your ideas, I shall sing to you."

The Vicar shuffled his feet in horror. They were large feet and made a lot of noise.

"Are you sure, my dear . . .?"

But she was off. The clear notes seemed to rise and hit the ceiling.

> *Put all your litter in the litter bin,*
> *And grin, grin, grin.*
> *Pick up your cartons and that old bean tin,*
> *Just pack that rubbish in.*
>
> *Save your paper and your string,*
> *To waste them is a sin——*
> *So pack all your litter in the litter bin*
> *And grin, grin, grin.*

Everyone clapped loudly. Pink and pleased, the Vicar's wife said, "Mr. Rab and I composed it this morning," and sat down. Tamworth rose to his trotters again.

"We must, of course, be clear as to whether we are trying to keep tidy or save waste materials."

"Both. Both," Mrs. Dench shouted enthusiastically. More people joined in.

"More litter bins."

"A paper collection."

"One at a time, please," called the Vicar's wife, but ideas were coming thick and fast now.

"A litter patrol."

"Competition for the tidiest garden."

"Flowers and trees planted everywhere."

In the midst of the excitement, Mrs. Baggs rose up to glare all about her.

"All I can say is that if you kept tidy like I do there'd be no need for all this rubbishy talk, for that's all it is, rubbishy talk. Come on, Christopher Robin."

In the sudden silence, they left, clompetty, clomp.

Then Mr. Starling, Thomas's teacher, put up his hand to speak.

"Has anyone taken a look at the old duck pond just past the Duck and Drake?"

"It's in a terrible state. Worse than the stream. I got quite a good rolling pin out of there, last week," cried

Mrs. Dench. Mr. Dench looked nervous, as well he might. It didn't do to argue with Mrs. Dench.

"I haven't seen it. I don't go near the Duck and Drake, you see," said Mrs. Twitchie. "Is it very bad?"

"Yes, indeed," Mr. Starling said earnestly. "And it's a shame for these old ponds to disappear, to die in fact, for they have played an important part in our history. Our village was probably built in the first place around that pond, for there would be water to drink and fish to eat."

"I know," said Tamworth. "It's a pleasant evening. Let's all go and inspect the pond in question, and decide what to do."

So all the people walked down the road to look at the duck pond. And they could see that Mr. Starling was absolutely right. It was like the ghost of a pond. Whitish scum clung round the rim where a few brownish grasses drooped.

"There, you see. The ducks and moorhens have left. The fish are dying. This year there were no tadpoles. Soon it will be just an old dump unless we save it."

They gazed in silence till, at last, Tamworth said:

"I suggest that we adjourn to the benches outside the Duck and Drake and there choose a Committee to run our tidiness campaign."

This was agreed, even by Mrs. Twitchie, and beer and cider, coffee and cheese, lemonade and crisps were handed round while Tamworth, the Vicar's wife, Mrs. Twitchie, Mr. Starling and Mrs. Dench were elected to be in charge.

47

"That's a jolly good way to have a meeting," Daddy said, joining them, late from work.

"I think Tamworth made it into a sort of party," Thomas said.

"Just a pleasant evening with friends," grinned the golden pig.

# Chapter Six

❖

Tamworth had begun reading lessons with the piglets and it soon became clear that they were going to be good readers with one exception. Albert made no progress at all.

"Don't want to read. Reading's silly. Albert too clever for reading."

Tamworth took no notice but held up a flash card with "Dog" on it.

"Dog," cried all the piglets, except for Albert, who shouted "Pig", in a very loud voice. Tamworth gave up flash cards for that day and read them a story instead. It was about an Iron Man and they liked it very much indeed.

"Albert going to write a story about an iron pig," announced that piglet.

"If you're going to write stories, it helps to be able to read," his father grinned.

Lessons over, Albert trotted out into the orchard, where the gate was open for once. Despite the fact that he had often been told not to go out on his own, he set off, pausing from time to time to push his snout into the ditch to find out if anything of interest was going on in

those murky depths. There was. A frog hopped on to
his snout and off again.

He decided to visit Thomas quite soon, but in the mean-
time it was simply great to be on his own for once, without
those other piglets who were really extremely stupid.

A little further along, on the bank, he spotted a plant,

a bit like that white, feathery stuff that Dad called Cow's Parsley. He sniffed it—he had a certain feeling—his fat little body quivered with excitement and he started to dig. Albert didn't know why. But pig ancestors across the years were telling him to dig.

There, at last, he found a large, brown root, smelling absolutely delicious and tasting like sweet chestnuts. Albert gobbled it down, his tail curling tight with delight. Yummy, yummy, yummy, oh bliss. Later, he'd ask Dad what it was but now, it was enough just to eat it. He dug up another.

Renewed and refreshed, he trotted on, black mischief in the bright morning, so full of happiness that, as he went along, he danced on his four trotters. He was Albert, and all the world belonged to Albert.

By now he was coming to houses and further on, pavements, and one or two people looked at Albert in surprise, but it was such a sunny morning that they were all in a good temper, so they just smiled and went on their ways. Farmer Baggs rode past in the Land-Rover, but Albert sat down, a fat shadow behind a telegraph post, and Farmer Baggs didn't see him.

Next, he came to Mrs. Dyke's shop and what should be just outside but a basket of apples. Like his father, Albert was partial to an apple. Just what Albert wants, thought that pig to himself, as he seized the biggest, and travelled rather more speedily along the pavement. But a hand fell on his back.

"And what do you think you're doing?" came a voice from above. "You're a thief." Albert tried to hurry on, and to hang on to the apple, but he couldn't get away from the hand. The apple was removed from his protesting jaws.

"Well, it's not much good, now. He might as well keep it. I suppose he's too little to know better." Mrs. Dyke patted him and said, "Now, go home, you naughty animal and never do that again."

Albert broke into a mini-gallop away from the scene of the crime and heard Mrs. Dyke say:

"I wonder if Tamworth knows that one of his litter is out on his own?"

By now Albert had passed the Duck and Drake and was nearing the pond, which had received a great deal of attention just lately, and was now looking much pleasanter and healthier as a result. And on its bank were two figures doing something with lines and rods and jamjars. Albert could see one bottom clad in plum-coloured corduroys and another in patched old jeans. The plum cords ended in bright pink socks.

Albert could not resist this. He dug his trotters into the ground, then thundered forward and butted the plum-coloured rear. There arose a terrible cry, followed by a loud splash which showered Albert and the other boy, who sat down, roaring with laughter.

"Help! Help!" cried the boy in the water. It was Christopher Robin Baggs, and Lurcher was the boy doubled up with mirth on the bank.

"I'm drowning," wailed Christopher Robin, standing up to his knees in the pond. Shreds of water-weed hung about him.

"You're all right," Lurcher gasped. "Just come towards me."

Then he saw Albert, and realized what had happened.
Leaving Christopher Robin to get himself out he moved
towards Albert, who backed away from him, being now
rather afraid of what he had done.

"Come on, now," Lurcher called, but Albert turned
to run. Lurcher grabbed him round the middle.

Albert squealed.

And out of the blue, appeared Thomas, eyes blazing
blue, face red with anger.

"What are you doing to Albert? Don't you dare hurt
him. Put him down!"

"I'm not hurting him. There we was, just minding our own business, checking the pond for Birdie Starling, when Albert comes along and pushes Baggsy in the pond."

Thomas turned and saw the miserable, wet figure stumbling up the bank, sobbing to itself.

"Come and help me, Lurcher."

Thomas and Lurcher began to laugh, stopped, then started off again.

"We ought to help him. Come on," Thomas managed to say at last. Mr. Starling had talked a lot lately about fair play and helping others, and Thomas liked Mr. Starling.

"I don't want you to help me. I don't like you," wailed Christopher Robin.

"All right. All right. I hate the sight of you, anyway. Lurcher, you take him home. I'll take Albert. Try and keep out of his mum's way."

So Lurcher went off with the wet and sorrowing Baggsy, while Thomas returned Albert home, singing at the tops of their voices, or rather Thomas was singing, while Albert squeaked in accompaniment.

Mrs. Baggs was very angry indeed, especially as the plum-coloured cords shrank and were never the same again.

"When are you going to get rid of those piglets?" she asked her husband.

"All in good time, Maud. When I've found the right homes for them. All in good time," he said, puffing peacefully at his pipe.

Someone else wasn't pleased either.

Tamworth had a quiet and private word with his son, and Albert was as quiet as a mouse and as good as gold for at least three days.

# Chapter Seven

❖

By now, everyone at school was interested in keeping the pond and the stream on the Common clear and un-polluted. Mr. Starling was in charge and each day a different class would visit them, unless the weather was too impossible, to clear away rubbish, watch the water life and make a survey of it. Fresh weed and snails and fish were added to the present inhabitants.

Trees and shrubs were planted on the village green by the Vicar. Periwinkle, snapdragons and forget-me-nots were set in banks and hedgerows. Tubs and window boxes were filled with plants and seeds. Tamworth tried to grow flowers outside Pig House, but they didn't do at all well because his piglets kept sitting on them. In the end he bought a fresh batch and put a fence round them.

Mrs. Twitchie organized the children into collecting rubbish from the village green, the churchyard, and the space in front of the Duck and Drake, as well as the playground and the school field.

The Vicar's wife collected milk-bottle tops and Mrs. Dench and her many children made a separate collection of waste paper. Tamworth put out posters and wrote to his friend the Minister for the Environment to come down in July to judge the best garden.

Life was busy.

Especially at school, which hummed with furious activity just like a beehive when the bees are swarming. For Open Day was approaching, that day when all the parents could come into school to see how their children were getting on. Art and Craft from Waste materials was one theme and the walls were hung with pictures made from bits of paper, oddments of wool and string, shells, buttons, straws, sand and tinfoil. Mobiles swayed in the breeze, and models made in clay, plasticine, polystyrene, egg boxes and toilet rolls stood in every space. A huge dinosaur, created out of newspaper papiermâché, startled any visitor entering the front door.

Mr. Starling had made a garden with his class, in which Thomas had planted a conker, now growing nicely. Lurcher had planted tomato plants, but the school tortoise had eaten some of them. Thomas's drawing of the giant oak tree in the middle of Tumbling Wood had a special place of honour on the wall. Blossom had three paintings on show, as well as her prize poster, and two poems. She had sewn a rag doll and helped to make a model castle.

Lurcher Dench's chief creation was a Viking sword and shield, cut out of strong cardboard, covered with tinfoil. Mr. Starling had persuaded him to keep it at school till Open Day, but when it was all over, he was going to take it home, and have a really good battle with someone, Thomas, he hoped. Thomas was a good scrapper, not at all like Christopher Robin Baggs.

Every child in the school had something to show as
well as their books and folders. Each class was doing a
display of some kind. Blossom's class was singing. She
had a violin solo. Christopher Robin was singing
"Joyous Bells Ring Clear" and Gwendolyn Twitchie
was playing the piano. Every dinner hour she practised
very loudly, so that the whole school knew her piece,
which sounded like this, "Twim frittering, twim
frittering, twimmer frittering."

Daddy asked what Blossom was singing this year, as he couldn't wait to hear it.

There was a laugh in his voice and Blossom, who always grew nervous and easily upset before any occasion, cried:

"You needn't come if you don't want to."

"Of course I'm coming. I wouldn't miss it for anything. What are you doing, Thomas?"

He muttered something under his breath and walked away. His form's effort was top secret. They were all excited about it and had done a tremendous amount of work. It was to be a complete surprise to the school and the parents.

Open Day arrived at last, to Blossom's sheer terror. At dawn she was up, practising.

"You beat the birds this morning," grinned her father, eating a hearty breakfast. Blossom refused all food, which showed how nervous she was.

"I didn't sleep all night," she said.

Thomas sat in silence. He was saying his lines over and over in his head, but he was determined that no one should realize this.

Before they set out for school it grew dark, thunder rolled, lightning flashed and the rain poured in torrents from a steel-grey sky. The white marking on the field was washed away.

"We needed rain," Mr. Starling said to his class, who were moaning and groaning about the weather.

"We didn't need so much that we all get drowned, or struck by lightning, sir," said Thomas.

"Never mind, it makes a good background for our

play. Come on, everybody, one last rehearsal, and take care that no one sees or hears you. Except us, of course."

"Are you sure no one knows, sir?" Lurcher asked.

"Pretty sure." Mr. Starling grinned.

Even the longest morning ends eventually, and at last it was afternoon. The rain stopped and patches of blue broke through the clouds so that the class who were to do the P.E. display outside kept running in and out to see how wet the grass was. But finally it was decided that it would be all right.

There the parents were led to sit on chairs, a little cold, a little damp, but clapping everything wildly, especially Crasher Dench, who could turn some of the best cartwheels ever, and who seemed to have rubber instead of bones inside him.

"I'm just as good as he is," Lurcher muttered jealously, as they watched from their classroom window.

"Yes, I know. But wait till they see our play. They'll really clap then."

"Time to get ready," sang out Mr. Starling.

The class assembled in a little room behind the hall, awaiting the signal to begin; a tremendous roll on the drums, followed by a very high note on the flute from Henry. As they waited they could hear the concert in the hall.

The reception class, the littlest ones, were singing, "I'm a little tea-pot, short and stout," followed by "Five little buns in a baker's shop."

"Stop whispering, and don't clink and clank," hissed Mr. Starling.

Their songs over, the babies were coming out to very loud applause. Suddenly the door opened and small faces looked in. The first one saw Thomas and Lurcher and burst into tears. The others turned and ran.

Mr. Starling looked a bit bothered.

"I hope we haven't made you too frightening," he said.

"I hope we scare everyone stiff," Thomas whispered to Lurcher underneath him.

The sound of a violin tuning up was heard.

"Lumme, I bet she makes an awful mess of it," Thomas groaned.

"Course she won't. She'll play well," said Lurcher.

And Blossom played very well, and so did Gwendolyn Twitchie. Then Christopher Robin sang, and Mr. Starling had to speak sharply to his class, who were all groaning. Then the choir lifted up their voices for "Lemon Tree".

"Get ready, are you all set?" Mr. Starling whispered.

"Down in Demerara," sang the choir.

"You all right?" Lurcher asked Thomas.

"All right, as long as you don't let me down!"

Mr. Starling looked as if he was leading his troops into battle. Henry picked up his flute. Children adjusted their masks and helmets.

And now was the moment. "Lord of the Dance" was drawing to its close.

"Go to it," breathed Mr. Starling.

The drum began to roll, slowly and softly at first, then louder and louder. And Thomas suddenly realized how nervous he was, and then he was nervous no longer, for the drum grew still louder, crescendoing mightily, louder than heart beats, louder than war drums, louder than thunder, till they stopped abruptly, and then— high and alone and clear and terrifying—came Henry's note on the flute.

Huge, perched up on Lurcher's shoulders into giant size, magnificent in his metal costume, made through patient weeks, eyes glaring through the slots in the gleaming helmet, Thomas stepped out from the back of the hall and shouted at the very top of his voice.

"We are the Iron Men! We have come to destroy you!"

Everyone in the hall swung round. There was a moment of complete silence.

Then someone screamed. It was the Vicar's wife.

More screams rang out as Thomas was joined by others in his class, dressed like himself as Iron Men, one mounted on another's shoulders.

"We must save the children," cried the Vicar's wife, leaping from her seat. It made a change from saving trees.

In the middle of all this, Thomas felt bewildered. He'd hoped to frighten them a bit, but this was ridiculous. And at that moment, a tremendous roll of thunder sounded above the hall. The storm had returned.

"It's the end of the world," Mr. Dench cried, scuttling for the exit. He was not at all brave. But Mrs. Dench hauled him back.

"It's only our Lurcher," she bellowed. "Told me about it, 'e did, though 'e wasn't supposed to. And that's Tim there wi' 'im." She always got his name wrong. "Now siddown."

Daddy was on his feet by now, speaking loudly to the people around him. "It's Thomas. Only Thomas. I'm sure it is. Now calm down."

But all was still confusion. Children were popping up

all over the place and shrieking at the sight of the figures. Mrs. Twitchie was trying to find her whistle.

"Do something," yelled Lurcher to Thomas.

Thomas lifted his sword and brought it down sharply on his shield.

"Silence. Sit down. We shall not harm you."

Then he lifted off his helmet.

The audience quietened down.

"Why, it's only Thomas. It's the children. Fancy that. Aren't they clever?"

Thomas put his helmet back on. Mr. Starling stepped forward smiling.

"Thank you for your appreciation," he said. "We shall now act a play, written entirely by the children."

They all remembered their parts. The Iron Men fought and defeated a country, but the people of the field and the forest rose against them and saved their land. Thomas and Lurcher died magnificently, with tremendous groaning, whirring and clanking. Thomas had been disappointed that they wouldn't be able to use tomato sauce for blood, for of course Iron Men didn't have any blood. The girls in green costumes danced a Triumph Dance at the end.

And the applause was absolutely fantastic. People cheered and clapped and shouted for Thomas and Lurcher and Mr. Starling.

"What a wonderful play," they cried to Mrs. Twitchie.

Back at home, Thomas sat quietly eating his tea. His family were looking at him, if not with respect, with something quite near to it.

"What I can't get over," his mother said, "is that you never breathed a word about it."

Blossom sighed. "You were wonderful. Much better than I could ever be."

"Not bad," Dad smiled. "I thought it was going to be a disaster, but you did well."

Thomas smiled modestly at his plate.

But later, when he went to see Tamworth who had not been able to come to school because of a meeting, he curled up beside the golden pig and said:

"Do you mind people who boast?"

"Depends who it is. No, I don't mind, sometimes."

"Can I boast to you, then?"

"Of course, dear boy. Boast ahead."

"Well, you see . . . there was this play that we did . . . and, Tamworth . . ."

"Yes, go on."

"I was absolutely brilliant."

# Chapter Eight

❖

After Open Day life was quiet and peaceful for a while. One warm Saturday afternoon Blossom was in the orchard playing with the piglets. From afar came the sound of Farmer Baggs haymaking. The air was full of summer. Bees hummed in buttercups which stood higher than the piglets. It was nearing tea-time and Blossom's thoughts lingered lovingly on the lemon cheese tarts and the cherry cake that her mother had baked that morning, for Uncle Jeff and Aunt Cynthia were coming to stay, as they usually did at this time of the year. Blossom had licked out the mixing bowl, yummy.

"I bet she's on a diet," Daddy said. He meant Aunt Cynthia, a tall skinny woman.

"She doesn't need to," said Mummy. "She's beautifully slim."

"She's like a filleted haddock. Now it's Jeff who will eat all the food, though he ought to slim, I think, because he's fat." Uncle Jeff was Daddy's brother.

"Did you quarrel when you were little, like Thomas and me?" Blossom asked.

"Much worse. But I always won," Daddy told her.

Blossom skipped round the kitchen, licking her spoon and singing:

> *I'm glad they're coming,*
> *Glad they're coming,*
> *Glad they're coming, hooray,*
> *Glad they're coming today.*

"Huh! I'm not. I hate them," shouted a voice in the doorway, and there stood Thomas, eyes like hot blue flames and hair standing on end.

"I don't ever want anybody coming to stay."

"Go upstairs to your room till you've learnt better manners," his mother said sharply.

"It isn't my room any more with that stupid girl coming in to share it. Fancy having to share a room with her."

"At least you're in your own bed in your own room. I'm in that old camp bed," Blossom cried.

"That's quite enough, you two." Mummy sounded so angry this time that Blossom went into the garden and Thomas went upstairs to Hedgecock and Mr. Rab.

"Grown-ups are never fair," he told them. "What a miserable life. Fancy having her . . ." he meant Aunt Cynthia . . . "mincing and being snobby all round the house. I might as well be dead or in a dungeon."

"When you're sorry, when you're sad, count your blessings and you'll be glad," warbled Mr. Rab, his pink nose quivering.

"What absolute poppycock," bellowed Hedgecock. "What's the point of counting blessings? First of all, with you around, I haven't got any, and second, the only things worth counting are numbers, glorious numbers."

And he started gabbling away to see if he could reach a thousand.

After a rather silent lunch, Thomas went off to visit Tamworth Pig, where he hid his face in the tufted ears before they went to inspect the stream together.

Blossom took the piglets to play in the orchard so that Melanie could have a rest. Albert had been full of mischief all the morning.

They played "Hide and Seek" and "Fire on the Mountain". Then Blossom lined them up at about ten yards' distance from her and sang out:

"Sheep, sheep, come home."

"We're afraid," cried all the little pigs.

"What of?" Blossom asked.

"The wolf," they answered.

> *The wolf's gone to Derbyshire,*
> *And won't be back for many a year.*
> *Sheep, sheep, come home!*

called Blossom, whereupon they all ran to a certain tree, which was home, and Blossom caught five little sheep.

"Let's make it pigs instead of sheep and Albert the wolf," suggested the piglet. So he was the wolf next. But he was so excited and dashed about so wildly that he didn't catch anyone, except Blossom who let him capture her. Then they had to play it again and again till they all flopped on the ground, puffing and panting.

Blossom managed to find them each a sweet, out of the emergency supply that she always carried, but she told them to keep it a secret because they weren't supposed to eat sweets.

"Tell us the story of the three little pigs," they cried. This was their favourite story (of all) and they were soon huffing and puffing and blowing houses in.

"If Albert ever met a wolf, Albert would gobble him up. Just like this," said Albert, biting Ethel's tail.

Ethel yelped.

"If you do that again, I'll send for that wolf myself."

Blossom's voice was stern, and Albert, the wolf-eater, looked terrified.

"Albert good pig, now," he promised.

"I shall have to go soon," Blossom told them. "Uncle Jeff and Aunt Cynthia are coming." The piglets pleaded for one more game.

"All right. Now I'm It and I'll catch you. If you touch a tree, you'll be safe, but you can only stay there as long as it takes to count three. Right, off you go."

As they ran off, Thomas appeared at the far side of the orchard, riding on Tamworth's back and holding on to the furry ears. From the other side of the orchard came Mrs. Baggs with a bucket full of eggs. Most of these eggs were the products of Ethelberta Everready, the ever-laying hen. Mrs. Baggs was shaking her head and muttering to herself, as she thought out ways and means of cutting down on the hen food so that she could get more profit on the eggs, when—

"Look out," Tamworth bellowed.

Mrs. Baggs looked up in surprise.

"Look out," cried Blossom.

Thomas did not cry out at all, but watched with glee as the round, black form, hurtling towards a tree, crashed into the egg bucket. Mrs. Baggs's woollen-clad legs wobbled. So did Mrs. Baggs. But she held her balance, though not the bucket, which flew out of her hand; eggs shot out everywhere. A gooey, yellow pool lay on the ground and in the midst of it bobbed two or three unbroken eggs. Albert's trotters slid from under him and he sat down, splosh. Mrs. Baggs stood there silently, spattered with egg yolks.

"What happened next?" asked Uncle Jeff, through a mouthful of cherry cake. They all sat round the tea-table,

sun streaming through the window. Mummy offered
cherry cake to Aunt Cynthia.

"Oh no, I couldn't possibly," she said in very refined
tones. "You see, I'm slimming."

Daddy grinned to himself.

"What did Mrs. Baggs do?" Uncle Jeff repeated.

"Well," answered Blossom, tucking into her fourth
slice, "Tamworth and I tried to clean her up, and rescue
the unbroken eggs, though there weren't many, but she
just stormed off in a temper. When she got to the gate,
she turned and cried, 'Tamworth Pig, I'll get you for
this', and went."

"I laughed and laughed and laughed," Thomas announced.

Aunt Cynthia looked at him in horror. She didn't like little boys. The only one she knew was Thomas, and she found him quite alarming and very peculiar.

But Uncle Jeff took him to one side and gave him a pound note.

"Go and buy yourself something. I like a good laugh," he murmured.

Aunt Cynthia allowed Blossom to try on all her make-up.

# Chapter Nine

❖

The visit of Uncle Jeff and Aunt Cynthia went off pleasantly. They thought that Blossom was very nice, and though Aunt Cynthia kept looking at Thomas as if he were going to explode, or erupt, or grow three heads, or as if he might turn into a mad monster from an alien planet, they didn't actually fall out over anything. And Uncle Jeff was generous with various sums of money, so Thomas decided he could put up with them after all, especially as he was at school most of the day, anyway.

On Saturday they went to see the lions at a stately home. The lions he liked, though he found them not a patch on Tamworth, but he didn't think much of looking at the house and furniture. He grew rather bored and told everyone so several times, in case they hadn't heard the first time. On the way home, he felt sick, and after he'd told them all about it, he was allowed to have the windows open. It had started to rain and had turned cold, but it was still better with the windows wide open.

When he got inside, he rushed up to see Hedgecock and Mr. Rab, who'd been left behind. Thomas thought this unfair and had said so. He'd said so quite often. As he ran up the stairs he heard his father say:

"That's the last time I'm taking him anywhere."

"I'll make a nice cup of tea for us all," Mummy said soothingly.

"That's jolly mean," muttered Thomas to his friends, as he draped Num all over the three of them, and settled down to read an ancient Beano. "I was all right. I can't help it if I don't like furniture. The lions were all right. I wonder if they belong to Tamworth's Union?"

About an hour later, they were all tucking into cheese pie and sausages, Thomas's favourite.

"No one would think, to look at him now, that he'd felt sick all the way home, would they?" said Aunt Cynthia in a peevish voice. "I've developed a stiff neck from that draught in the car. I think you spoil him," she went on.

Thomas glared at her. The end of the sausage, speared on his fork, fell off and landed on the floor. He bent down, dusted it off and pushed it into his mouth. Aunt Cynthia shuddered and put down her knife and fork.

"I think I shall go up to bed. I really don't feel very well . . ." but at that moment there came a banging on the door and in rushed Melanie, trembling all over, eyes wild.

"Are they here?"

"Are who here?" asked Mummy.

Thomas knew what Melanie meant. "The piglets? Is anything the matter?"

"They've gone. I did so hope they would be here, safe and sound."

She broke into loud sobs. Mummy patted her.

"Tell us what happened."

The sobbing quietened and Melanie started to explain. That day Tamworth and Farmer Baggs had been invited to an important meeting about conservation, and they'd left early in the morning and would not be returning till late. The Vicar's wife had called on Melanie during the afternoon to ask her if she'd give a talk about the problem of rearing twenty children. Melanie had said yes, and then since it was a warm afternoon . . .

". . . It was cold in the car," interrupted Aunt Cynthia, and everyone went "Sh."

"They were all sound asleep," Melanie continued, "when I went out, looking like angels, they were, even Albert. But when I got back, there was no sign of them, anywhere, not even a bristle. And I've searched and searched but they've gone. Vanished completely. . . . And I came to you. . . . Oh, where are they? And what will Tamworth say?"

She collapsed, a sad black and pink heap on the floor.

"Where did you search?" Daddy asked.

"In the orchard, through the farm, along the road. I went to see Mrs. Baggs but she wouldn't speak to me. She never has spoken to me. She just tossed her head and walked away."

"That's just like her," cried Thomas.

"How long were you talking?"

"Only about half an hour. But that was long enough for someone to kidnap my babies."

"Pignapped. They've been pignapped," Thomas shouted. "Come on, let's go and search everywhere."

"We'd better report to Constable Cubbins, I think,"

Daddy decided. "Thomas and Blossom, go and search everywhere you think they might be. Take some of your friends with you to help."

They set off to search, full of excitement and alarm. Mummy brewed some tea and gave a drink to Melanie. "We'll soon find them, don't you worry," she said.

But by nightfall the piglets were still missing. Nor had Farmer Baggs and Tamworth returned home.

# Chapter Ten

---

An enormous lion was standing over Albert.

"I'm going to eat you up," the lion roared.

"Oh, no, no, no, you're not," Thomas shouted. "I'm coming, Albert. I'll save you."

Thomas was running to rescue Albert, running and running, but the lion and Albert came no nearer. The ground began to shake under his feet. It shook and shook so much that Thomas woke up to find Blossom shaking him.

"What's up? Don't let them eat Albert, will you?"

"That's what I've come about," Blossom whispered. "I've got an idea."

"What?" Thomas sat bolt upright, wide awake at last.

"Sh. We don't want to wake Mummy and Daddy up. I want us to do this ourselves. Listen."

"I am listening. Shut up, Hedgecock." Hedgecock was snoring like a hive full of bees.

"Remember Mrs. Baggs's brother? The one who lives on the road about a mile beyond Tumbling Wood?"

"Yes."

"Well, I've suspected Mrs. Baggs from the first. I

know she hated the piglets and couldn't wait to get rid
of them. And I think that with Tamworth and Farmer
Baggs and Melanie out of the way, she seized her
opportunity, and got someone to take them away. And
I think it would be that brother of hers. He's got a big
garden, with a shed in it. I might be wrong but I think
the piglets are in that shed. And I want to go and find
out. Now."

Thomas started to pull on his clothes.

"I've got a torch," Blossom said.

"Let's go," Thomas said. "I'm not scared."

"I am," Blossom shivered, "but I'm still going."

Thomas picked up Num and wrapped it like a scarf around his neck.

"If I'm going through the Tumbling Wood at night, I'm having Num with me even though I'm not a bit scared," he explained.

"I've got some chocolate," replied Blossom.

They whispered farewell to the snoring Hedgecock and whiffling Mr. Rab, neither of whom took the least notice. Then they made their way downstairs, softly, softly, and into the kitchen. Gently they drew back the bolt and went into the garden.

Blossom had feared the darkness of the night. But it was light. The moon seemed to be galloping through the sky, trailing long cloud streamers. Shadows were outlined clearly on the ground; the garden shed, the trees, Daddy's wheelbarrow were as visible as if it were day. Blossom looked at her watch.

"It's half-past midnight."

"Come on," answered Thomas. "We've a long way to go."

They ran to the Common, where the stream glinted in the moonlight, and the trees spread their shadows on the grass.

"It's like another world," panted Blossom, and——

"Tu-whit, tu-whoo," hooted in their ears.

"Oh," Blossom screeched, terrified.

"It's Owly. Hello, Owly," cried Thomas.

Wings flapped low over their heads in reply. They ran on.

Ahead loomed a monstrous shape with a huge shadow. A sinister low moan came from the shape. Blossom stood still, shaking.

"I'm going home. I'm just not brave enough," she whispered. The monstrous shape came nearer.

And Fanny Cow mooed gently at them. Blossom flung her arms around her.

"I thought you were a monster," she cried.

"No, I'm a moo-cow, not a monster," Fanny lowed. "Where are you going?"

"We're going to find the piglets. They're missing."

"I know. Everyone knows, except Tamworth and Farmer Baggs and he hasn't come back yet. Joe is with them. Where do you think they are?"

"I think Mrs. Baggs's brother, Bert, has taken them, because Mrs. Baggs was so anxious to get rid of them."

Fanny chewed her cud ruminatively.

"Come to think of it, I did see his van leaving the farm this afternoon."

"I knew it," Blossom cried. "Come on, let's go."

"Which way?" Fanny asked.

"Over the Common, through the Rainbow field and up to the Tumbling Wood, and out on to the road beyond. Then it's about half a mile along the road. It's a long way," Blossom sighed.

"I'll come to the edge of the wood with you," Fanny offered.

"And so will I," came a voice behind them, and there, looking impressively fierce in the moonlight, stood Barry MacKenzie Goat.

"I'm not at all scared now," Blossom laughed.

"I wasn't scared anyway," Thomas boasted.

Blossom pulled a face at him, but he didn't see, which was just as well. By the side of the stream little heads popped out.

"Good hunting," called the Chief Mole.

"Good hunting," answered the band of rescuers.

On they went through the moonlit lanes and fields until ahead of them loomed the dark mass of Tumbling Wood. As they approached the trees a small animal lolloped towards them, the Welsh Rabbit, Mr. Rab's friend.

"It was Owly told us you were coming, he did, so to meet you I came, for it is that all the animals of the wood are for you watching out, this night, because it was you helped Tamworth to save the trees and our homes. They will not be seen by you, but watch over you they will. Good luck go with you."

He flipped his ears at them, then turned and vanished into his hole under the elderberry bush, as the children followed the path into the heart of the wood. It seemed enchanted; the ferns and the flowers and the trees shone silver. Far away an owl hooted. Owly was busy. Further away still the sharp cough of a fox was heard. Up and through the wood they went, past the huge oak tree, which Thomas called the tree of Saint Thomas, but which Blossom thought of as the King of the Wood. They reached, at last, the edge of the trees on the other side. Mrs. Baggs's brother, Bert, lived further along the road.

The two animals stopped and said:

"We'll wait for you here. Good luck, friends."

Fanny bent her neck and nibbled the soft grass. Barry turned to some tender shoots in the shadows.

The children walked on in silence, the road unwinding itself before them, like a long white ribbon. Although they had come quite a distance, they were not tired. Their feet moved effortlessly as in a dream. Everything was still. They might have been alone in the world. Blossom shivered.

And there ahead was the house, standing alone in its large garden. Two windows were watching them, like eyes. Thomas gathered Num more firmly around him. Blossom ate two pieces of chocolate. Then they reached the hedge, and slowly crept along beside it. They arrived at the gate and pushed it open cautiously. It creaked, a sharp, frightening noise in the silent night. A dog, somewhere in the garden, started to bark. Thomas and Blossom stood still as statues, hearts pumping loudly. After a moment a light went on, a window was flung up, and a face looked out.

"What is it?" asked a voice in the room behind.

"I don't know," the man at the window answered.

The dog barked frenziedly. The children stood frozen, not daring to move forwards or backwards. And then came the hoot of an owl, right above their heads, followed by the rush of wings.

"Shut up," shouted the man to the dog, and threw something at him. The dog subsided, growling low in his throat then fell silent.

"It's only that old owl again," said the man. The window dropped down and the light went out.

Blossom and Thomas moved silently to a small, dark, shadowy building in the corner of the garden.

"Do you think they'll be there?" whispered Thomas.

"I don't know. I might have been wrong."

Blossom felt unsure now. Suppose she had made a stupid mistake and they'd come all this way for nothing? All at once, she felt tired and nervous. Thomas moved ahead of her.

And from inside the shed there came a faint eek.

# *Chapter Eleven*

❖

Like a streak of lightning Thomas shot to the shed door, and tried to open it.

"It's padlocked," he hissed at Blossom. From inside came yet more eeks, then——

"Let Albert out," called a well-known voice.

"Shush!" whispered the children through the door. The dog started to growl again.

"I need something to open it. A screw-driver," said Thomas as quietly as he could, but the piglets heard his voice and started to eek once more. Trotters skittered inside.

"We'll get you out, but for Pete's sake, shut up!" Thomas's voice was hoarse with desperation, as he pulled at the lock. Blossom pulled at his arm.

"I've found a key. It was in an upside-down flower pot. I knew that was the sort of place people leave keys."

But Thomas wasn't listening. He turned the key in the lock.

The door swung open, and twenty little pigs overflowed into the moonlit garden. Thomas waved his hands at them.

"Follow me. And be quiet!"

He led the way as softly and quickly as he could to the gate. They were almost there, when Ethel squealed sharply. Albert, pushing his way to the front, had trodden on her.

The dog began to bark as loudly as if he had three heads, each one giving voice. Lights went on. The window opened, and a head looked out. Someone shouted.

"Run for your bacon," Thomas yelled at the top of his lungs. The time for silence had gone.

Through the gate and on to the road ran the piglets, little legs pounding like pistons. Thomas was in the lead; Blossom kept with the slowest at the back, a terrified Blossom, yet full of anger at the pignappers.

Doors banged, footsteps sounded and curses flew through the night after them. Trotters clattered on the moonlit road where the piglets ran, a bobbing mass. If we can only reach the wood, the animals will be there, with their protecting horns, thought Blossom. But now they were out on the open road and the wood seemed miles away. Behind them a van started up, revving furiously.

"Oh, hurry, hurry," Blossom cried. The many trotters speeded up a bit, but the piglets were tiring, Ethel lagging behind the rest. Blossom picked her up and tucked her under one arm, though her own legs were aching cruelly and a stitch stabbed her side. Thomas was forging well ahead with Michael and Albert. Headlights shone from behind, lighting up the road, the little pigs and the children.

"They're going to catch us," Blossom sobbed in-

wardly. "It's too far to the wood. Oh, I wish someone
would come."

The van was coming up rapidly now, overtaking them.
A new fear struck Blossom, that the driver might run
over them in his rage. Her breath came in sharp, hurting
pants. Ethel jogged up and down.

But there was another car, other headlights, approaching them. And then it seemed that following their
pursuer was yet another car, the sound of a horn and
more headlights again: noise and brightness all about

them. She looked behind her. The van behind was dwarfed by a tall vehicle, with blazing lights. The piglets rushed forward in terror almost under the wheels of the approaching car. But it had stopped and getting out of it was the completely comforting form of P.C. Cubbins. He bent and picked up Albert, who had taken the lead.

Suddenly, above everything else, the piglets' yelps and squeals, the screech of tyres and brakes, there sounded a roar deeper than that of any lion, louder than thunder.

"What are you doing to my children?"

Into the middle of the road strode Tamworth, as big as a house, as tall as a tree, and leaned over the kidnapper's van. From within there came a cry of terror, the door flew open, and away, back down the road, ran Bert, Mrs. Baggs's brother as if demons were after him.

"I'll catch him," Farmer Baggs cried. "I'll get him. I've never liked the rascal."

He ran down the road, followed by Joe the shire horse galloping along. Joe had been travelling in the horse box, the tall vehicle that Blossom had seen.

P.C. Cubbins put Albert down again.

"They won't take long to catch the villain. I'll get out my notebook ready."

"Dad," squeaked all the little pigs. "Dad."

Tamworth sat down in the road and they all swarmed over him, licking and sniffing and nuzzling him and all talking at once.

"We were pignapped."

"Nasty man came with Mrs. Baggs."

"Nasty man and nasty van. Albert bit nasty man," boasted that piglet.

"Nasty dark shed. No supper."

"Then Thomas came. And Blossom. Then we ran."

"Albert very brave pig."

"I think you were all brave, especially Blossom and Thomas," Tamworth said, getting to his trotters and trying to move them to the horse box. Hooves clattered down the road. Blossom cried, "It's Fanny and Barry," as they approached, and from the other direction, came Farmer Baggs seated on Joe the shire horse, with Bert placed in front of him, terrified.

"I think it's time to go home," Tamworth Pig said.

P.C. Cubbins drove the captured Bert to the police station, while Farmer Baggs took the others home. Mummy and Daddy were surprised to see their children in the early hours of the morning. But they didn't say much, only put them to bed, where they fell asleep and didn't wake up till late. On the other hand Farmer Baggs had a great deal to say to his wife when he got home.

But later he spoke up for Bert and promised that he would be a law-abiding citizen in the future.

"You see, 'e's one of the family," he explained, "and it's me duty to look arter 'em even if they're a rotten lot at times."

# Chapter Twelve

❖

The village bloomed as spring changed to summer. Window boxes, tubs, borders, gardens frothed with flowers. Visitors came to view the village green and the churchyard. The duck pond revived through loving care; plants and fish and birds returned there. The stream on the Common continued to flow freely. Mrs. Dench rolled into action like a giant bulldozer and made all her family tidy the garden and grow flowers and vegetables in it. Some of the rubbish she dumped in the attic, the rest over the high hedge at the bottom of the garden. It was worth the effort; the Denches won the prize for the best-kept garden. This annoyed some people but everyone was pleased when the village came fourth in the "Keep Britain Tidy" competition.

The piglets grew and grew. Thomas once more visited the lions, but on a school trip this time. Gwendolyn Twitchie was terrified when a lion came to the coach window where she was sitting and grinned at her in a hungry fashion. Thomas wasn't sick on the way home but three other children were. It was just the usual sort of school outing, in fact. Lurcher Dench climbed on the school roof after a ball for the two hundredth time, but this time he fell off and broke his arm. It was put in plaster and everyone wrote their names on it. It stopped him bowling, but he did manage to bat one-handed.

And the piglets grew and grew and grew. The day came when there was to be a farewell party for them before they left for the good homes carefully selected by Tamworth and Farmer Baggs.

On the evening before this party Thomas wandered to the Common and lay in the grass on the edge of the stream. He lay and watched the water flowing past and listened to it singing its song. The sun was slowly setting in a golden sky. Tomorrow would be a sunny day. Tomorrow there would be a picnic in the orchard for the piglets.

Thomas contemplated the minnows in the stream. A huge shadow fell over him. Tamworth had arrived. He lowered his enormous bulk on to the ground beside Thomas, who put an arm round him as far as he could. Thomas sighed. Tamworth sighed. At last Thomas said sadly:

"Why do things change? Why can't they stay the same for ever and ever?"

"Everything changes, Thomas. It's the way of things. 'Tempora mutantur, nos et mutamur in illis.' "

"Eh?" grunted Thomas.

"Latin, my dear boy. The times change and we change with them. The piglets grow up and have to go. There's hardly room for them in Pig House any more."

"I don't want anything to change. I want it to stay like this for ever and ever."

91

"You'd get very bored. Come on, let's check the stream. We've done a good job here."

They walked slowly along. There beneath a tree stood Blossom with Joe. She was just feeling in her pocket and bringing out a sugar lump for both of them. When she saw Tamworth tears sprang to her eyes.

"Suppose they're lonely without us? I can't bear to think of it."

"Look," said Tamworth, "suppose we all cheer up. They're not going miles away, and we shall see them again. Come on, Thomas, up on my back and let's race Joe to Pig House. An hour with Albert will make you happy he's leaving."

"Giddy-up, Tamworth," yelled Thomas.

It was a splendid picnic. They all ate and sang and enjoyed themselves, even Christopher Robin Baggs and Gwendolyn Twitchie, whom Blossom invited, though Thomas grumbled. There were no tears even when Farmer Baggs brought the Land-Rover round to take the piglets away.

"Remember to keep up with your reading."

"Remember to say please and thank you."

"Come back and see us."

Melanie kissed them all good-bye. People went away. Tamworth and Melanie, Blossom and Thomas, Hedgecock and Mr. Rab sat in the strange quiet the piglets had left behind them. They sat still for quite a while.

"I think we'd better go home, now," Blossom said at last.

A peculiar noise came from the cupboard in the corner.

"What's that?" Blossom cried.

Thomas rushed to the door and pulled it open.

"Albert's here," shouted that piglet, trotting into the room, grinning from ear to ear, tail tightly curled.

"But you've gone," gasped Melanie.

"Albert popped in big car one side and came out the other, then hid in cupboard. Albert clever pig."

Tamworth looked stern.

"This clever pig had better get ready to go, once more."

"Let him stay. Let him stay," cried the others.

"Albert can't read yet. Better stay till he can," said Albert meekly.

"Let him stay," shouted the others.

"You're outnumbered, Tamworth," grunted Hedgecock. "Bad luck."

"All right. I give in. You may stay for a while, though I shall undoubtedly regret my weak decision. You've got to behave, Albert, and you've got to learn to read."

Albert looked saintly.

"Albert good pig," he said.